Dear Phoenix,

Everyplace I go I think about you. We will have fun exploring together when you are ready to travel.

Love,

Sammy

P.S. Pepe thinks you will like to play in the sand & jump in the waves

To plants, animals and kids everywhere.
We all have a lot to learn from one another.

— MP

Gulf
of
Mexico

U.S.A.

T h e
B a h a m a s

C u b a

G r e a t e r   A n t i l l e s

Cayman Islands

Jamaica

Honduras

Nicaragua

Costa Rica

Panama

Colombia

Caribbean Sea

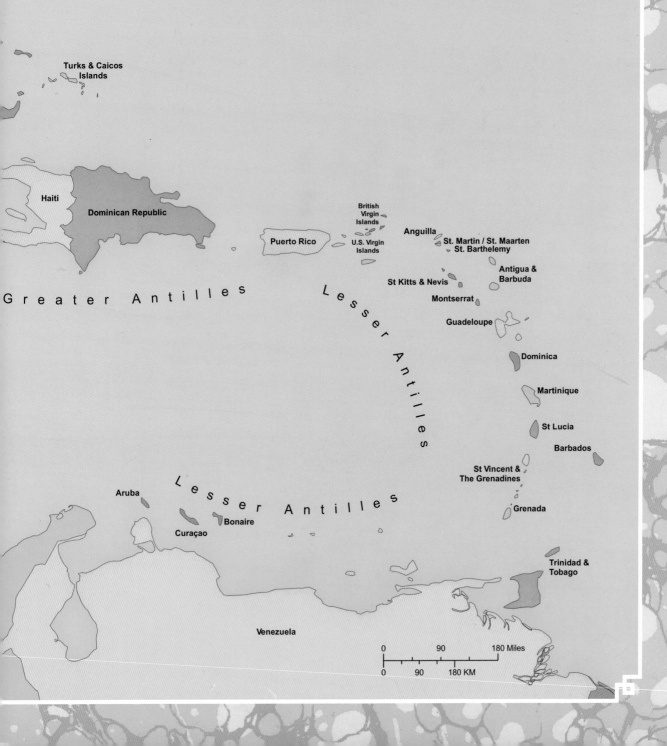

Atlantic Ocean

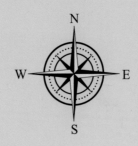

Turks & Caicos
Islands

Haiti

Dominican Republic

G r e a t e r   A n t i l l e s

Puerto Rico

British
Virgin
Islands

U.S. Virgin
Islands

Anguilla

St. Martin / St. Maarten
St. Barthelemy

Antigua &
Barbuda

St Kitts & Nevis

Montserrat

Guadeloupe

L e s s e r   A n t i l l e s

Dominica

Martinique

St Lucia

Barbados

St Vincent &
The Grenadines

Grenada

Aruba

L e s s e r   A n t i l l e s

Bonaire

Curaçao

Trinidad &
Tobago

Venezuela

| 0 | 90 | 180 Miles |
| 0 | 90 | 180 KM |

For more information regarding permission, write to
Little Bell Caribbean
P.O. Box 236
West Hurley, NY 12491

Visit us online at www.littlebellcaribbean.com
To see more of Cherise's artwork, visit www.cheriserward.com

Book design by Yolanda V. Fundora / www.urban-amish.com.
Patterns throughout the book are from her licensed textile collections.

The Library of Congress has cataloged the paperback edition as follows:

Picayo, Mario, 1957-
[Fables. Selections]
The shark and the parrotfish and other Caribbean fables / by Mario Picayo ; illustrations by Cherise Ward.
pages cm
Summary: Provides a Caribbean twist to classic fables from Aesop and La Fontaine,
featuring such creatures as hermit crabs, dolphins, and manatees. Includes facts about the animals.
ISBN 978-1-934370-36-0 (pbk.)
1. Fables. 2. Tales--Caribbean Area. [1. Fables. 2. Folklore--Caribbean Area.] I. Ward, Cherise, illustrator.
II. Aesop. III. La Fontaine, Jean de, 1621-1695. IV. Title.
PZ8.2.P453Sh 2014
398.209729--dc23
2013046328

ISBN-13: 978-1-934370-38-4

Manufactured in China

9 8 7 6 5 4 3 2 1

The Shark and the Parrotfish and Other Caribbean Fables

Written by Mario Picayo
Illustrated by Cherise Ward

Contents

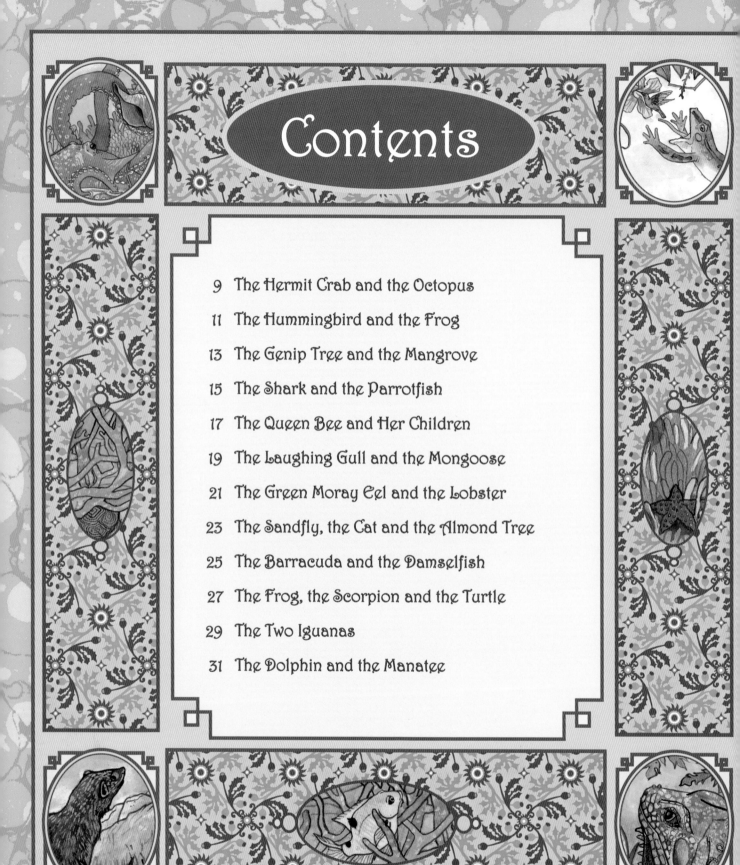

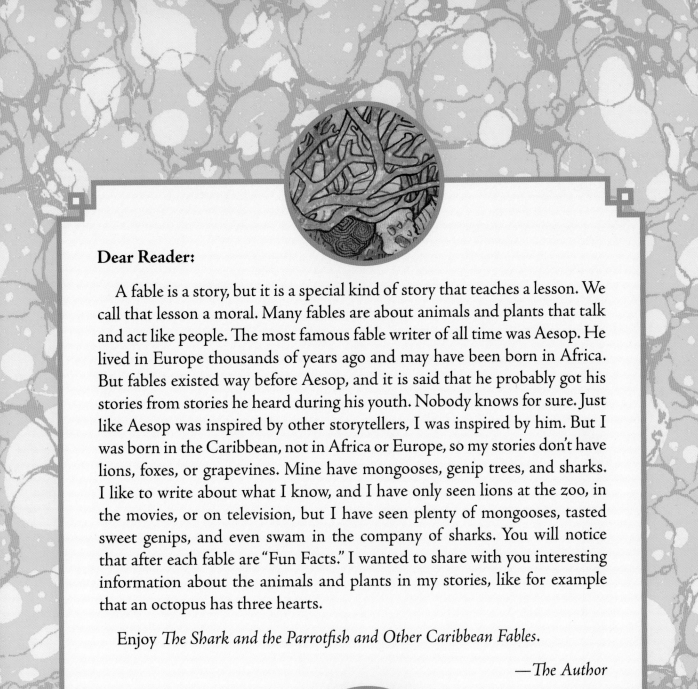

Dear Reader:

A fable is a story, but it is a special kind of story that teaches a lesson. We call that lesson a moral. Many fables are about animals and plants that talk and act like people. The most famous fable writer of all time was Aesop. He lived in Europe thousands of years ago and may have been born in Africa. But fables existed way before Aesop, and it is said that he probably got his stories from stories he heard during his youth. Nobody knows for sure. Just like Aesop was inspired by other storytellers, I was inspired by him. But I was born in the Caribbean, not in Africa or Europe, so my stories don't have lions, foxes, or grapevines. Mine have mongooses, genip trees, and sharks. I like to write about what I know, and I have only seen lions at the zoo, in the movies, or on television, but I have seen plenty of mongooses, tasted sweet genips, and even swam in the company of sharks. You will notice that after each fable are "Fun Facts." I wanted to share with you interesting information about the animals and plants in my stories, like for example that an octopus has three hearts.

Enjoy *The Shark and the Parrotfish and Other Caribbean Fables.*

—*The Author*

The Hermit Crab and the Octopus

An old Hermit Crab, who had not visited the ocean since he was young, decided to walk to a nearby reef and smell the sea air. His shell was old, too, and he was going to need a new one very soon. As the Hermit Crab got closer to the sea, *sploosh!* a wave washed over the rock, and even though he held on tight, the Hermit Crab's shell came off and disappeared under the sea. "Oh, no! My shell is gone! What am I going to do?" he cried. Not a minute had passed when he saw, right next to him, one tentacle, two tentacles, three, four, five, six, seven, eight tentacles! An Octopus had come up from the ocean floor and was staring at him. "Are you going to eat me?" asked the Hermit Crab. "No," said the Octopus, "I am going to help you. What is the matter?" "I lost my shell. It is my shelter, my protection!" cried the old Hermit Crab. "Is that all?" answered the Octopus. "I will get it for you." And *bloop!* down he went into the water.

In no time at all, the Octopus was back with a pink shell as smooth as silk. "Is this your shell?" asked the Octopus. "No," said the Hermit Crab, "that is not my shell." "Alright," said the Octopus, and *bloop!* down he went again into the water. He returned with a beautiful orange and green shell that shined like the sun. "Is this your shell?" asked the Octopus. "No," answered the Hermit Crab, "that is not my shell." "Alright," said the Octopus, and *bloop!* down he went again into the water. This time, he came back with an old beat-up shell, thin from use, and with chipped edges. "That's the one!" exclaimed the Hermit Crab with joy. "Why do you like this old shell?" asked the Octopus. "Because it is mine," said the old Hermit Crab. "I would rather sleep in my old shell than in a brand-new one that might belong to somebody else." "Your honesty should be rewarded," said the Octopus. Into the water he dove one more time and returned with a bright blue and gold shell with little glowing dots that looked like stars. "This one is mine," said the Octopus, "and I want to give it to you." It was the most beautiful shell the old Hermit Crab had ever seen. After thanking the Octopus, the old Hermit Crab put the shell on and smiled all the way home.

Honesty should be its own reward, but sometimes it is also rewarded by others

Fun Facts: The **Caribbean hermit crab** (*Coenobita clypeatus*) is a crustacean that lives from central Florida and south throughout the Caribbean. They are born in the ocean and, when young, can be found along the shore. Later in life they can live far from the sea on dry land. Every August through September, thousands of hermit crabs return to the ocean to lay eggs. Like in the story, hermit crabs move from one shell to another as they get bigger. The **octopus** is one of the ocean's most fascinating creatures and ranges in size from tiny to gigantic. Some species carry coconut shells and seashells to use as protection. Octopuses have three hearts and eight "arms" or tentacles, can change colors, produce ink to escape danger, and can also move by "jet propulsion" by expelling water at high speed.

The Hummingbird and the Frog

A Hummingbird was happily hovering and drinking nectar from a flower near a pond when a Frog leapt and *gulp!* grabbed the tiny bird in her mouth. The Frog was ready to eat the Hummingbird, when suddenly she heard a little voice speak, "Please don't eat me! Let me go and I'll fly far away and you'll never see me again." But the Frog replied, "No, I love eating insects. They are my favorite food in the whole world!" "Insect?" asked the Hummingbird. "Wait a minute, this is a big mistake! I am not an insect. I'm a bird! Can't you see my feathers, or my beak?" "But you are so small," said the Frog. "Birds normally try to eat me! Not the other way around." "I understand your confusion," said the Hummingbird. "I am very small, but I am a bird." The Frog thought about it, and after a few seconds decided to let the Hummingbird go.

Not a week had passed when the Hummingbird was drinking nectar from a beautiful pink flower near the same frog pond. Suddenly, a different Frog leapt and *gulp!* caught him in its mouth. The Frog was ready to swallow his catch when he heard the Hummingbird yell, "Let me go, Frog, and I'll fly, far, far away and you'll never see me again!" "No!" said the Frog, "I love eating birds, and I don't get to catch a bird very often." "A bird?" asked the Hummingbird, "I'm not a bird, I'm an insect! Can't you see how small I am, and how I was hovering just like my cousin the dragonfly?" The Frog remembered that it had never seen a bird that small, or one that could hover. "Alright," said the Frog, opening his big mouth, "you can go. I really want to eat a bird today and don't want to spoil my appetite on an insect." As soon as the Hummingbird was out of the Frog's mouth he flew away as fast as he could and never went near a frog pond again.

✆ **Think fast and don't push your luck**

Fun Facts: Frogs have been seen eating hummingbirds. Green frogs, which are quite fast, seem to be especially good at hummingbird hunting. How small can a **hummingbird** be? Cuba's bee hummingbird (*Mellisuga helenae*), the smallest bird in the world, is only two inches tall—about the size of a bumblebee and smaller than a dragonfly. By the way, hummingbird brains are very small because the birds are so small, but their brain-body ratio is larger than that of most animals, including humans.

The Genip Tree and the Mangrove

One windy afternoon, a tall, strong Genip Tree, famous for the sweetness of her fruits, saw not far from the hill where she lived a group of trees she had never noticed before. They were right on the shore and living in swampy, salty water. "You down there!" said the Genip Tree. "You picked the worst place to settle in. That's salt water, you know? And what is that sticking out of the sand, your roots? I bet that even a little breeze will send you flying. I mean, are you even a tree?" "We are Red Mangroves," said a tree of small branches and roots that seemed to grow above the sand instead of under. "We are trees and we will be fine here," he said. "Well," said the Genip Tree, "you'd better be ready, because a hawk just told me that tonight the winds will be strong enough to change the shape of the land. I am big and in good soil, and have nothing to worry about, but I am sorry for you since you will be under seawater by morning." Just as the hawk had told the Genip Tree, the winds blew stronger and stronger as the night got darker. Large trees began falling left and right of the Genip Tree. Even her best friend, a Mango Tree so old that no one could remember a time when she wasn't there, fell with a thunderous *CRASH!* when a powerful gust struck her. The beautiful Genip Tree saw her own limbs snap, leaves and fruits fly away, and branches break off as if they were little twigs. She survived only because she was slightly off the path of the mighty hurricane that crossed the island from side to side. The sun rose the next day and destruction was everywhere. The bruised, half-broken Genip Tree woke up, gazed towards the ocean, and felt the breeze that was salty and soft as a whisper now. She looked down to the swamp, and to her surprise there were the Mangroves, just as the day before, as if nothing had happened. "I am the biggest fool in the world," she said, "and I am sorry for my pride. You, that look so little and weak, have done better than most of us, who are ten times your size."

☙ **Do not judge anyone by their size, their looks, or where they live**

Fun Facts: Genip (*Melicoccus bijugatus*) is a large tree that produces small sour-sweet fruits. It is known by many different names, such as genip, kenep, skinnip, ackee, and quenepa. You can find genip trees as big as eighty feet or taller. The **red mangrove** (*Rhizophora mangle*) is a type of tree that, unlike most other trees, can live in salty water. Mangrove thickets (many plants together), are home to all kinds of animals and are very important to coastal areas. The propped roots of the mangrove stick out and give the tree a very unique look, plus protection and balance. **Hurricanes** are tropical storms with consistent wind speeds of seventy-four miles per hour or more. Hurricanes carry heavy rain and winds powerful enough to take down trees and even houses. The Caribbean has a "hurricane season" from June 1 to November 30, but hurricanes can form at other times of year, too.

The Shark and the Parrotfish

A Nurse Shark could not fall asleep because of a Parrotfish's constant crunching on coral. Fed up, he swam to the Parrotfish and caught him in his jaws. He was about to eat him up, when the Parrotfish cried, "Please don't eat me! If you let me go, I will repay the favor someday!" The Nurse Shark smiled and said, "There is no way you can ever repay me for your life, but you made me smile with your nonsense, so I'll let you go." It just so happened that a few days later the Nurse Shark was caught in a fisherman's net. He tossed and turned and tried as hard as he could to escape, but all he did was get more and more tangled. The Parrotfish recognized the Nurse Shark and gnawed the net with his teeth until the Nurse Shark was able to escape. "You laughed at the idea that I could ever help you," said the Parrotfish. "Now you know that even a powerful shark can use the help of a small fish like me."

❦ **It is always good to have friends, no matter how small they are, or how big you are**

Fun Facts: **Nurse sharks** do sleep. It was once believed that all sharks had to swim constantly in order to breathe and could not sleep for more than a few minutes at a time. Nurse sharks have spiracles that force water across their gills, allowing for stationary rest. Sharks do not sleep like humans do, but instead have active and restful periods. **Parrotfish** are considered to be herbivores, but they eat a wide variety of reef organisms. Their pharyngeal teeth grind up coral rock during feeding. After digesting the rock, they excrete it as sand, helping create the sandy beaches of the Caribbean. One large parrotfish can produce 200 pounds of sand each year! You can actually hear the grinding if you are underwater near a parrotfish when it eats.

The Queen Bee and Her Children

A Queen Bee had a family who were always fighting among themselves in the beehive. She tried again and again to solve their arguments, but they would not listen to reason. One day a large Orb-weaver Spider moved near the entrance to the hive, so that every time a bee flew out on her way to the nearby flowers, *zoop!* she would get stuck in the Spider's web. The arguments in the hive were getting worse and worse, so the Queen Bee decided to teach her children a practical lesson.

"Go out to the garden," she commanded one of her daughters, who dutifully flew out, only to get caught in the Orb-weaver Spider's web. "Now you," she told another young bee, and this one also flew out of the hive also getting stuck in the web. "See how that Spider is catching your sisters one by one?" she asked the bees gathered around her. "That is what happens when you act alone. Now," she said, "all together, fly out and go to the flowers in the garden." The bees, hundreds of them, did as they were instructed and flew into the web. Together they were so strong that the Orb-weaver Spider's web broke easily into a thousand threads and released the trapped bees. When the family returned to the hive, the Queen Bee spoke to them: "My children, if you act together and help each other you will be stronger than your enemies, but if you are divided among yourselves, you will be easily defeated."

🐝 **There is strength in numbers**

Fun Facts: The **honey bee** (*Apis mellifera*) is a popular and important insect, since it produces and stores honey. Honey bees can give a painful sting if bothered, or while defending their hive, where they live. In Mexico and Central America, honey is traditionally obtained from a native stingless bee (meliponine) as well as from the "regular" honey bee. **Orb-weaver spiders** make the very beautiful spiral webs that you see in most gardens and forests. Some species do catch honey bees on their webs, but honey bees are not a very important part of their diet. There are more than 10,000 species of orb-weaver spiders in the world.

The Laughing Gull and the Mongoose

A Laughing Gull was standing on a tall pole near the beach, ready to eat a piece of bread that he had found. A hungry Mongoose saw him from below and said to herself, "I would love a piece of that bread, but I am sure that Laughing Gull is not going to share it with me." So the Mongoose decided to trick the Laughing Gull. She got very close to the pole, looked up, and said, "What kind of bird are you? Your feathers are gorgeous! You must be the best-looking bird in the world. If your voice is as handsome as you, I will tell every animal I know that I met the king of all birds. Why don't you sing a little song for me?" The Laughing Gull, who had never heard such praise for his looks, opened his beak to sing, and *plop!* the piece of bread fell to the ground where the Mongoose was quick to grab it. "You are a good-looking bird," said the Mongoose, "but you need to be less vain and a little smarter."

☙ **Be mindful of praise**

Fun Facts: The **laughing gull** (*Leucophaeus atricilla*) is a medium-sized gull common in North America and the Caribbean. As the name implies, they are very vocal and their call sounds like a series of laughing notes. Laughing gulls often live very near people, and they will eat bread and other human food. A **mongoose** (*Herpestes auropunctatus*) is a small carnivore that has been introduced into most of the larger Caribbean islands from its native South Asia. In the wild they eat insects, birds, and other small creatures, but mongooses can also become scavengers and eat human food, like the piece of bread in our story.

The Green Moray Eel and the Lobster

A Green Moray Eel, tired of hunting for food, decided to try another way of getting his meals. He lay in his cave on the reef and pretended to be so sick that he could not move or hurt anyone. Many fish felt bad for their neighbor, and went in to say goodbye, only to be gobbled up by the Eel. A Spiny Lobster that had been watching from behind a rock figured out the Moray Eel's trick and decided to pretend she believed him. She walked over to the entrance of the cave and said, "Hello? Inside? Moray Eel? How do you feel?" A sickly voice from the cave answered, "Not well at all! I am getting weaker by the minute. Why don't you visit me for a little while?" "I am sorry to hear that you are not well," said the Spiny Lobster. "We are going to miss you around here." The Moray Eel stuck his head out of the cave, and looking at the Spiny Lobster said, "You are acting very shy. Come inside so we can chat." But the Spiny Lobster knew better and answered, "Sorry, old friend, I'll stay out here and not for much longer. Many fish have gone in since early morning, and I am still waiting to see the first one come out."

☙ **Paying attention can keep you out of trouble**

Fun Facts: The **green moray eel** (*Gymnothorax funebri*) is a moray eel found from New Jersey, on the eastern coast of the United States, all the way to South America. Like in the story, moray eels mostly wait for prey to come to them, instead of actively hunting. They eat fish, mollusks, and even lobsters. Green moray eels can look scary with their sharp teeth and snake-like shape, but they are shy animals and harmless to people, unless bothered or threatened. They can be as long as eight feet and weigh more than fifty pounds! And they are not really green. Their bodies are brown, but yellow mucus that covers them makes them look green. The **spiny lobster** (*Panulirus argus*) is a nocturnal crustacean found throughout the Caribbean, the northern coast of South America, in the Gulf of Mexico, and elsewhere in the region. It lives among underwater rocks and corals that offer protection from the many creatures, including their greatest threat: humans.

The Sandfly, the Cat and the Almond Tree

A Sandfly landed on a piece of fish that had washed up on the beach, when a Cat arrived and began eating the tasty treat. The Sandfly flew away saying, "What does that Cat think? He has no right to make me move. I will teach that big bully a lesson." The Sandfly flew close to the Cat's ear and said, "Listen, you, I am not afraid of any big Cat! I will prove to you that I can beat you in a fight fair and square." The Cat, who did not understand the language of Sandflies, only heard a buzzing noise and flicked his ear, tapping the Sandfly by accident on one wing. "Oh! So that's the way you fight!" yelled the Sandfly. "Now you really leave me no choice but to teach you a lesson." The little Sandfly flew straight for the Cat's nose and *zing!* bit him with all her might. The Cat swung his right paw, trying to move the pesty insect away, but the Sandfly was quick and flew out of the way. The Sandfly kept moving, *bzzz!* and biting the Cat. *Bzzz! zing! bzzz! zing!* Finally the annoyed Cat grabbed the piece of fish and left the beach. "Yes, run away you coward!" said the Sandfly. "I don't ever want to see you around here again." The Sandfly was tired and decided to fly over to the shade of an Almond Tree nearby, but she wasn't paying much attention and got stuck on a big spider web. "Oh, no," she cried, "I, the mightiest of animals, who can defeat a Cat, will be eaten by a little spider." She had not finished speaking when, *plop!* a big almond fell from the tree, breaking the spider web and freeing the Sandfly. "Aha! So now it is YOU who wants to fight ME," the Sandfly said to the Almond Tree, "throwing big almonds at me while I am tangled in a spider web and can't defend myself? I will teach you a lesson that you will never forget!" The Sandfly began flying from branch to branch, *bzzz! zing! bzzzz! bzzz! zing!* biting leaves and fruits with all her might, while the Almond Tree continued to enjoy the hot afternoon sun, not feeling a thing.

✦ **Sometimes you see enemies where there are none**

Fun Facts: The **sandfly** (or sand fly) is a tiny insect that lives on beaches and can be very annoying to humans and other animals with its painful bite. It belongs to the order Diptera, which includes mosquitoes, gnats, and flies. Only the females bite, and they don't do it to be annoying or look for a fight, but because they need the protein in our blood to make their eggs. I don't need to explain what a **cat** is, but I can tell you that cats have lived with humans for around ten thousand years, and that they are one of the most popular pets in the world. The tropical **almond tree** (*Terminalia catappa*) is a large tropical tree found in many beaches and coastal areas. It can tolerate salty spray, sandy soil, and strong winds. The tree is planted for shade, its edible nuts, and its wood, which can be used for furniture or lumber.

The Barracuda and the Damselfish

A big Barracuda, known in the coral reef as a bully, saw a Threespot Damselfish farming her algae plot and thought, "I am not really hungry, but I'll eat that little fish for lunch, and I'll tell her that she deserves to be eaten for things she has done to me." But the Barracuda was lying and the Damselfish had done nothing wrong. "Hey, I know you!" shouted the Barracuda. "Last year you bit my tail." "Me?" answered the Damselfish, surprised. "I was only born this year." Then the Barracuda tried another lie. "No, I remember now. You are the one who steals my food!" "What? No, no, you are confused," said the Damselfish. "I don't eat fish. I eat only algae." The Barracuda tried one last lie. "Well, you shouldn't swim in MY ocean!" "*Your* ocean?" said the Damselfish. "The ocean is not yours, and even if it were, I never get to swim anywhere since I can't leave my garden plot." The Damselfish had not finished talking when *zoom!* the Barracuda swam toward her at full speed with razor-sharp teeth showing. But the little fish was quick and hid behind a staghorn coral where the Barracuda could not reach her. "How did you know I would try to eat you anyway?" asked the Barracuda. "Ha!" laughed the Damselfish. "I've heard about you and knew that you could not be trusted and would try to eat me no matter what."

Bullies will find an excuse for their actions, even if you have done nothing wrong

Fun Fact: The **threespot damselfish** (*Eupomacentrus planifrons*) is a small, tropical reef fish. As in the fable, threespot damselfish maintain algae gardens. They eat the polyps from the coral so that the algae can grow and then they protect it, help it grow, and eat it like any farmer would. Their favorite coral is the **staghorn coral** (*Acropora cervicornis*), a threatened species. Damselfish will fight much bigger fish like parrotfish to protect their algae farm. The **great barracuda** (*Sphyraena barracuda*) is a long torpedo-shaped fish with very sharp teeth that can be found in the Caribbean and other parts of the world. Barracudas are normally three to four feet long, but can be bigger, and are very fast swimmers. They feed on fish, so if given the chance a barracuda would definitely eat a damselfish.

The Frog, the Scorpion and the Turtle

A young Frog was sitting at the edge of a river, when out of nowhere a Scorpion landed on his back. "Take me to the other side of the river, or I'll sting you!" she demanded. The Frog got very scared because he knew that a Scorpion's sting was very painful. "If I take you, you won't sting me?" asked the Frog. "That's right," lied the Scorpion, who was planning to sting the Frog and have him for supper as soon as they got to the other side. The Frog did not believe the Scorpion, and he came up with an idea to save himself. "Wait," he said. "You see my friend the Turtle over there? She is a much better swimmer than me, and the current is strong today. Why don't you let her take you?" The Scorpion saw the Turtle, who looked like a much bigger meal than the Frog, and said, "Very well, take me to her." The Frog did as told and, arriving at the Turtle's side, said, "Hi, Turtle, my friend the Scorpion needs a ride to the other shore and I think you should help us, being a much better swimmer than me." The Turtle was wise and understood right away what was going on. "Sure!" she said. "Get on my back." The Scorpion did as told, and the Turtle got into the water and began to swim. The river was wide but the Turtle was a good swimmer and had no problem reaching the other shore. As soon as the Scorpion felt safe, *wham!* she slammed her stinger on the Turtle's shell, but no matter how hard she tried, the stinger did not go through. "You can keep trying if you want," said the Turtle, "but you will not hurt me. Now get off me quickly before you end up where you started." The Scorpion got off the Turtle and before leaving the shore said, "I didn't get to make a meal out of either of you, but you did me a favor by bringing me over. This is where I live. I drifted on a piece of wood and had no idea how to get back to my family." It was getting late, so the Turtle wasted no time and began swimming back. The water was calm and everything was quiet and still. As the Turtle reached the middle of the river, she heard two voices that sounded like echoes. "Thank you," they said. One voice came from the Frog, the other from the Scorpion.

☞ **Be smart, be careful, be good, be grateful**

Fun Facts: **Scorpions** are arachnids, meaning that they are related to spiders. If you see one, you will notice the pair of claws and the tail ending in a poisonous stinger. They can give a painful sting, but generally they hide and are not harmful to humans. Scorpions will eat just about anything, including insects and, yes, even frogs. They are not swimmers but can stay underwater for hours and not drown. **Frogs** are amphibians and known as great swimmers and jumpers. You can find frogs near freshwater, whether a puddle, river, swamp, or pond. Frogs start their life as eggs, then become fish-looking tadpoles. When they are tadpoles they eat mosquito larvae, and later as frogs they eat mosquitoes, so they are helpful animals. **Turtles** are reptiles and like to stay near water. Most of them have hard shells, but some turtles have soft shells. There are sea turtles and freshwater turtles. The one in our story is a freshwater turtle, probably an Antillean slider such as *Trachemys terrapen, Trachemys decorata,* or *Trachemys stejnegeri.*

The Two Iguanas

A very young Iguana was basking in the sun on a rooftop. He decided to walk on a clothesline between the roof and a nearby papaya tree in order to reach the young leaves and ripe fruits. But as soon as he set all four legs on the clothesline, his hind legs slipped and he found himself hanging by his front claws at a considerable height. "Help! HELP!" he screamed. An old Iguana, hearing the commotion, arrived and looking up, began scolding the youngster. "What's wrong with you? Only a fool would try to balance on such a thin rope! You should have come down from that roof and climbed up the tree. You can hurt yourself acting like that, you know? See what happens to the lazy?" The young Iguana, who was getting tired from hanging, replied, "I understand what you are saying and appreciate your concern, but I need you to push that pile of hay so that I can safely jump down, and then you can scold me as much as you want."

In times of need advice is good, but help is much better

Fun Facts: Iguanas are large lizards that live in many Caribbean islands. You can also find iguanas in Central and South America and other regions of the world. The most common iguana that you will find in the Caribbean is the green iguana (*Iguana iguana*). Like in the story, iguanas love to eat leaves, flower buds, and fruits. Basking in the sun is important for iguanas since it helps increase their body temperature and aids digestion. They are also excellent climbers.

The Dolphin and the Manatee

A very fast Dolphin was swimming across a bay when she saw a Manatee gently grazing at the bottom of the shallow waters. The Dolphin approached the Manatee and said, "I've been watching you, and you must be the slowest creature in the ocean. I think you are slower than a sea star!" The Dolphin continued with laughter in her voice, "You are so slow that I could probably swim around the world before you get to the end of this bay!" "I am faster than you think," said the Manatee. "Oh, really?" said the Dolphin. "Do you think you are faster than me?" "I can probably beat you in a race," answered the Manatee. "Don't make me laugh!" exclaimed the Dolphin, swimming in fast circles. "Ok then," said the Manatee, "let's have a race. The first one to reach Pelican's Rock at the far end of the bay is the winner." "Great!" said the Dolphin. "This is going to be fun." "I'll be the judge!" said a Stingray who was swimming nearby. As soon as the Stingray said, "On your mark, get set, GO!" the Manatee began swimming at his normal slow pace, while the Dolphin zoomed away at full speed. She swam so fast that in less than one minute she was in the middle of the bay. "This is boring," the Dolphin thought. "That slowpoke is going to take forever to get here. I'll go play with that fishing boat out at sea and be back with plenty of time to win." The Dolphin reached the fishing boat and playfully jumped, flipped, and ate as many fish as the crew tossed overboard. So much jumping and eating made her very tired. "I guess I have time for a nap," said the Dolphin, and in no time she was fast asleep. A while later she woke up and, realizing she had overslept, swam as fast as she could. But as she reached Pelican's Rock, the Dolphin saw the Manatee ahead of her, crossing the finish line. "I declare you the winner!" said the Stingray to the Manatee. The Dolphin could not believe that she had lost. The Manatee, as slow as ever, swam over to the Dolphin and said, "I may be slow, but I never stopped. And that, my friend, always wins the race."

☙ **The race is won not by the fastest, but by the one that never stops**

Fun Facts: The **West Indian manatee** (*Trichechus manatus*), also called a sea cow, is a gentle giant (up to 14 feet and 1,300 pounds) found in Caribbean waters, frequently near rivers. They are plant eaters, feeding on water grasses, algae, and weeds. Manatees, like dolphins and whales, are mammals and need air to breathe. They do move slowly, at around five miles per hour, but can move faster when needed. The **common bottlenose dolphin** (*Tursiops truncatus*) is found in most oceanic waters, as long as they are warm. They eat fish but will also eat shrimp, squid, and octopus, and, like in the story, they do follow fishing boats to see what might be tossed overboard. Dolphins sleep by resting one-half of the brain at a time! It's called unihemispheric sleep. And they are fast, reaching speeds of more than fifteen miles per hour.

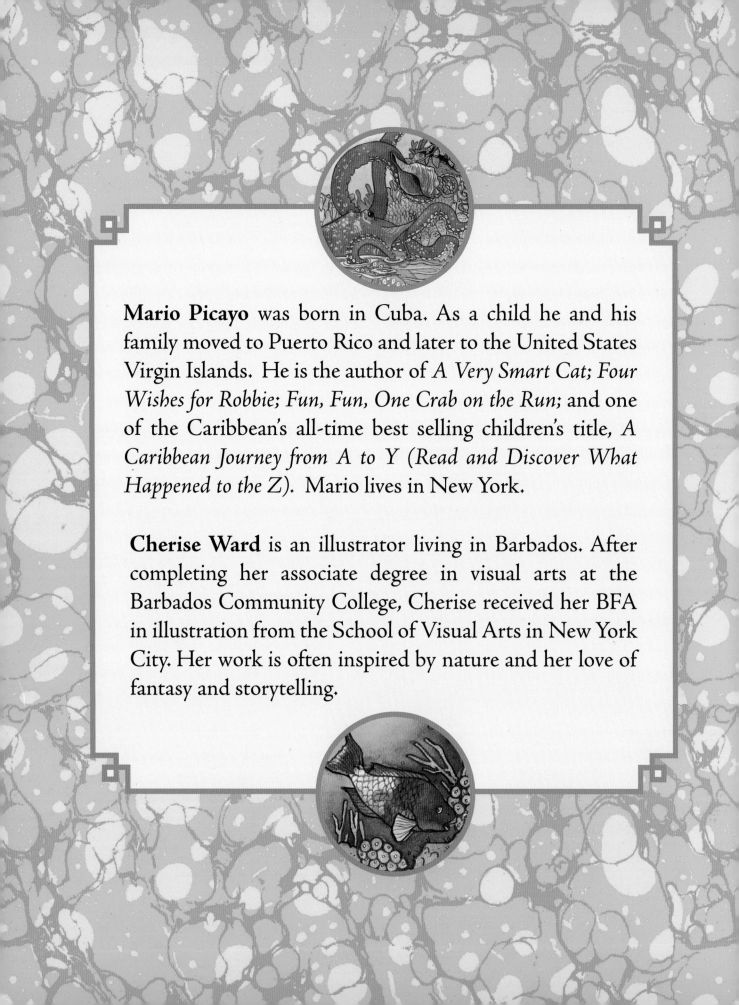

Mario Picayo was born in Cuba. As a child he and his family moved to Puerto Rico and later to the United States Virgin Islands. He is the author of *A Very Smart Cat; Four Wishes for Robbie; Fun, Fun, One Crab on the Run;* and one of the Caribbean's all-time best selling children's title, *A Caribbean Journey from A to Y (Read and Discover What Happened to the Z)*. Mario lives in New York.

Cherise Ward is an illustrator living in Barbados. After completing her associate degree in visual arts at the Barbados Community College, Cherise received her BFA in illustration from the School of Visual Arts in New York City. Her work is often inspired by nature and her love of fantasy and storytelling.